For John and Katya Ivie, two winners ~ R. W.

For Max ~ A. R.

Text copyright © 2002 by Rick Walton
Illustrations copyright © 2002 by Arthur Robins

First U.S. edition 2002

Library of Congress Cataloging-in-Publication Data

Walton, Rick.
Bertie was a watchdog / written by Rick Walton ; illustrated by Arthur Robins.
p.   cm.
Summary: Bertie, a dog as small as a watch, outsmarts an overconfident robber.
ISBN 0-7636-1385-1
[1. Dogs—Fiction. 2. Size—Fiction. 3. Robbers and outlaws—Fiction.]
I. Robins, Arthur, ill. ii. Title.
PZ7.W1774 Wat   2002
[E]—dc 21   2001037893

10 9 8 7 6 5 4 3

Printed in China

This book was typeset in Klepto ITC.
The illustrations were done in watercolor and ink.

Candlewick Press
2067 Massachusetts Avenue
Cambridge, Massachusetts 02140

visit us at www.candlewick.com

BERTIE WAS A WATCHDOG

illustrated by

Rick Walton   **Arthur Robins**

CANDLEWICK PRESS
CAMBRIDGE, MASSACHUSETTS

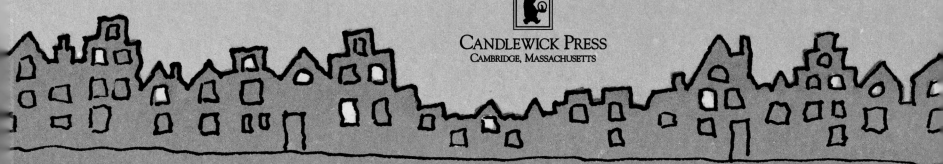

Bertie

was a watchdog.

But Bertie wasn't called
a watchdog because
he was big, or mean,
or scary.

He was called a watchdog

because he was about the size

of a watch.

Bertie
was a **very**
small dog.

So when a horrible robber
came into the house,
late one night,
and saw
Bertie . . .

"Ha, ha! What a tiny dog!" said the robber. "I'm not afraid of you."

"Why not?" said Bertie.

"Because you probably bite like a fly!" said the robber.

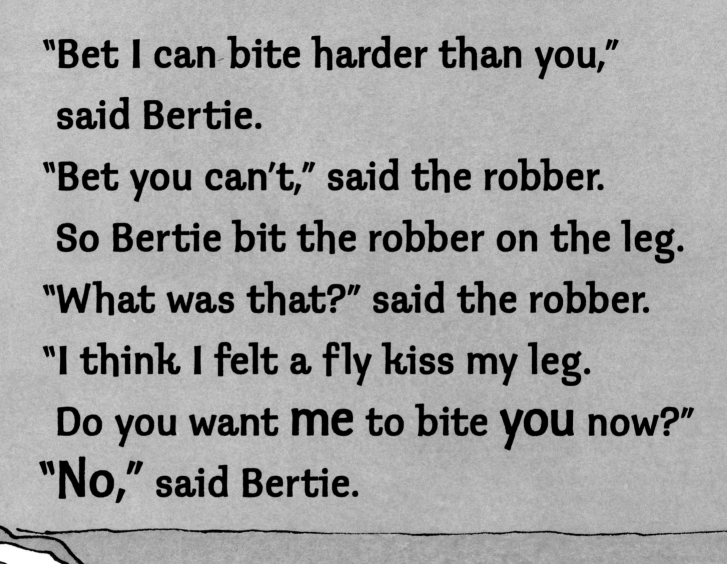

"Bet I can bite harder than you," said Bertie.

"Bet you can't," said the robber.

So Bertie bit the robber on the leg.

"What was that?" said the robber.

"I think I felt a fly kiss my leg.

Do you want me to bite you now?"

"No," said Bertie.

But the robber bit Bertie anyway.

"Yeow!"
said Bertie.
"Ha!" said
the robber.
"I win!"

"Bet I can chase you and catch you," said Bertie.
"Bet you can't," said the robber.

Bertie chased the robber around the sofa.

Finally Bertie stopped running.

"I win, I win, I win!" said the robber. "Though you're pretty fast . . .

for a **turtle!**"

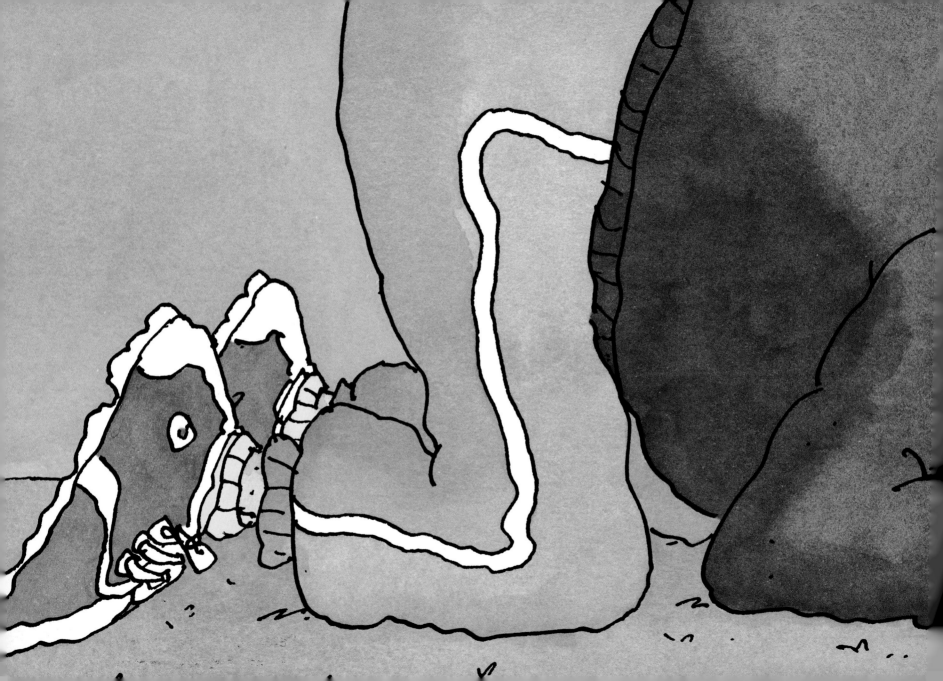

eeep!

barked Bertie.

HA HA!

HA!

HA!

A HA

"HA HA HA! Just as I thought," said the robber. "You're not a dog, you're a **mouse!** Let me show you how a **real** dog barks."

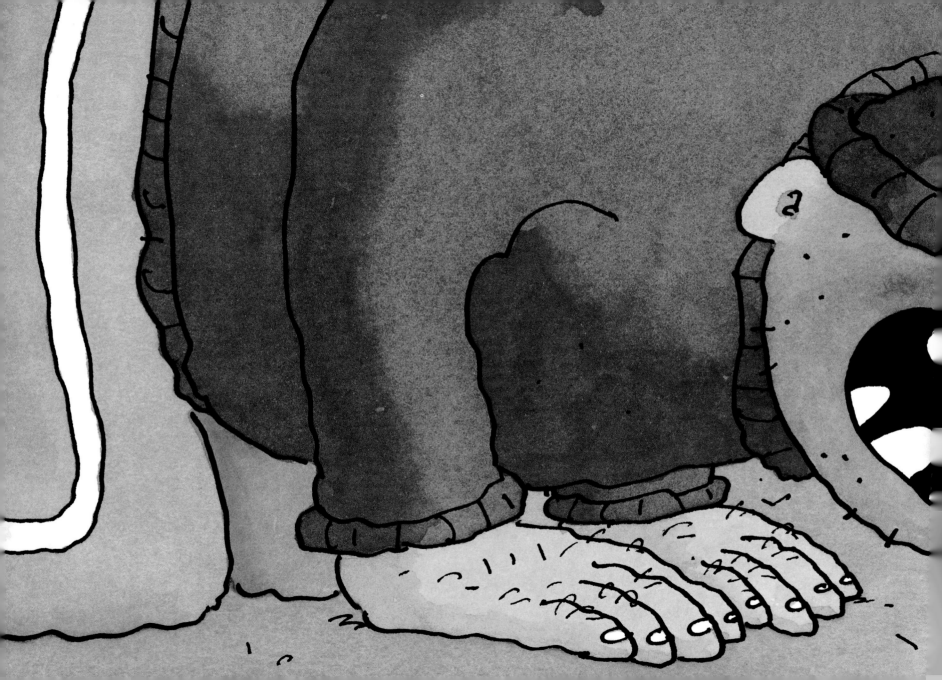

And the robber took a deep breath, bared his teeth, and shouted . . .

ARF ARF ARF ARF ARF ARF

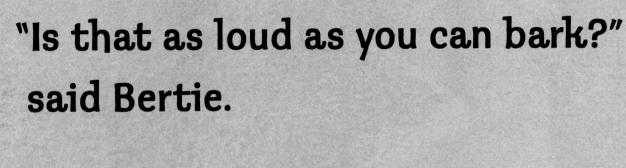

"Is that as loud as you can bark?" said Bertie.

"You don't think that was loud?" said the robber.

"Well, listen to this. . . ."

ARF ARF ARF RUFF RUFF ARF

WWWWEEEEEEEEEEEEEEEEEEEEEEEEEEEE

Just then the door flew open.
It was the **POLICE!**

"It's him!" they shouted, and they chased the robber around the sofa . . .

and caught him,
and handcuffed him.

"We heard your barking, little dog," the sergeant said, "and came to investigate. We've been looking for this robber for a long time. You're a **hero!**"

Bertie grinned
at the robber
and said . . .